I0819964

OTHER WORLDS

I. RILEY PEAK

OTHER WORLDS...

and their stories

Published by
S.C. TreeHouse LLC
183 Parker RD
Benton TN, 37307
books@sctreehouse.com

Stories By: J. Riley Peak
Illustrated & Edited by: Christopher D. Stewart

DEDICATION FROM THE EDITOR-

For my best friend Riley.
You made this book possible...but only because you didn't finish the other one I planned to publish.

&

For Kimberly. You made a good double agent during the publication of this.

-TABLE OF CONTENTS-

-INTRODUCTION-

The question regarding whether or not other planets share earth's unique ability to rear life is a question many ask. However, because men much smarter and consequentially more handsome than I have undertaken this very thing to no avail, I resign myself to the idea that I must leave such a search alone. Despite my lack of credentials in this field, though, there is, in fact, another discussion to which I can speak. For I can speak of worlds, and why bother talking about planets when one can speak about worlds?

From the time humanity first filled its lungs with breath, we have looked to the skies for other worlds. It has only been recently that the smartest of men thought to look down instead of up. Indeed, I myself have discovered worlds both above and below. The problem is not where they're looking; it's what they are using to look with. You can't observe them with your eyes. You can't see the scent of a rose, nor can you watch the internal shattering of someone's heart. Like sound or emotion, there are indeed other worlds—ones both deep, dark, and mysterious as well as light, high, and hopeful. Both the smell of a flower and the throes of despair are real experiences; we just don't see them with our eyes.

The Havenport Project

By: J. Riley Peak

Original Prologue

By: J. Riley Peak

Over-population: for years it had been a nagging worry in the back of leaders' minds. Soon it began to take shape as a nuisance; then it progressed to a concern; eventually, it became a global epidemic. An increasing number of people meant there was a shrinking amount of land available for them to sustain themselves on. One day an idea was brought, the premise of which was rather straightforward: there's much more water surface than land surface on the Earth; if we can build cities on the water, then we will have plenty of room for people and free up all the land for crops and produce. Soon after its presentation, the idea was seized upon, and the Planning Committee was established to see every detail was thought through. The project was called Havenport. It was to be a self-sustaining outpost—with its own city government, marketing districts, utilities, and scientific development departments. It was intended that once established, the city would make corrections and new developments on their outpost; all the Planning Committee had to do was give them a strong start. It was a time of hope when this city was first built, and there had been little trouble in finding willing volunteers to pioneer this new floating city. But it was feared that hope would die in its infancy when, merely two years after its establishment, a great storm came and broke the anchors that held Havenport in its predetermined coordinates. Free of its moorings, the port was driven before the storm into colder waters. This posed the double threat of freezing both the people of the city and the machinery that allowed Havenport to remain above its aquatic terrain. In the midst of this peril, a young member of the scientific research department stepped out to solve the task. His name was Ezekiel Era, and he, along with his wife, Nora, braved the storm to rescue the city. Through a clever readjustment of the gravitational machinery, they were able to save the city. However, that salvation came at a cost. Nora became deathly ill after the arduous task in the brutal weather. She passed, leaving Ezekiel to raise their young son, Eli.

For years, the promise of Havenport gleamed brighter than ever, and life was prosperous. However, now, eighteen years into an increasingly less than promising future, a new dilemma has struck the city.

The Havenport Project

Night had settled over Havenport. The stars, like lantern-bearing nomads passed overhead in the darkened sky. It was a moonless night, which caused the stars to stand out even brighter; their soft light bleached the city skyline with a ghostly pallor. This, along with the eerie stillness of the hour caused the city to appear dead. However, the stillness was defiled by a lone figure, bounding across the rooftops, his outline muted against the night sky by his dark outfitting. Like some phantasmal apparition, the figure seemed to leap effortlessly from one building to the next; it was as though gravity was having difficulty keeping a hold on this dark-clad figure, only pulling him back to earth when it could catch sight of him. As he continued his course, the figure stole a glimpse at the starry sky above him, wondering at the fact that people on the mainland could not enjoy such a beautiful sight. He had been told that the sky there was obscured by pollutants, due to the mass concentration of industry and machines there.

Eventually, he reached the east side of the city. There, he perched on a roof that positioned him across from the windowed-face of a tall apartment building. This was the part he always dreaded: picking the target.

Behind each of those windows was a home and a family just trying to do the best they could with what they had. He removed his mask, revealing the face of a young man, and he sighed. It always bothered him: why should these have to suffer for his plight? It wasn't their fault.

"But then," he thought, "whose fault was it, anyway?"

Most people blamed the Planning Committee, but the young man felt that that was not a fair thing to say—you can't blame someone for something they didn't even know would happen. Honestly, how could anyone have predicted the economic disaster?

It had been a year since it happened. It began with The Stagnation of the Scientific Department, which soon after came crashing down. This left an entire department without work and sent them out into the city in search of new jobs. The problem arose, in that Havenport, being a stand-alone unit, was very limited in its economic sectors; it was not prepared for such an event. The Planning Committee had painstakingly calculated the numbers and formulas to ensure that Havenport's economy could function at a rate corresponding with the approximate population growth of the city; they had not calculated that one of those segments should collapse. Thus, many were left without work. This included the young man's father, Ezekiel Era.

Ezekiel's troubles had started before The Stagnation (as it was called). At that time, just before all of this began, Ezekiel had contracted a mysterious degenerative disease—believed to be connected to the elements he had been experimenting with at the time. Ezekiel applied his mind to finding a cure but was met with mixed results. He found treatments which could slow the degenerative effects to a crawl but nothing to stop them. Thus, even as the Scientific Department succumbed to the effects of degeneration, Ezekiel Era engaged in a rebellion against his own similar fate. Often he chased possible antidotes for weeks, only to find them useless or, as on one occasion, poisonous. Ezekiel's illness left him unable to go out in search of work, thus that responsibility fell to his only son, Eli.

Now, here was Eli, standing on a lonesome rooftop, sizing up which apartment he was about to break into. It wasn't an ideal situation. Of course, Eli had tried to find honest work, but like many other unfortunates within this city, he was unable to secure anything. Thus, he had to make a desperate turn—thievery. Eli didn't, in any way, savor the prospects of surviving by this means, but he did it—and continued to do it—out of necessity; he had to provide until his father could recuperate.

Eli spotted a promising window, about five floors up from his current location. He stepped up onto the edge of his current roof to get a better look. It was slightly open, which wasn't entirely surprising; one typically doesn't have to worry about such things when they live on the twenty-third floor of a building. Eli put his mask back on and checked to make sure his boots were ready for the leap. They had been the key to this whole operation—and perhaps the first thing he had ever stolen.

The boots were a prototype designed by his father as little more than a pet project, but he had been unable to finish them and they had been residing within his closet ever since. They were made to reduce the pull of gravity upon an individual, designed using the very same technology that propelled Havenport above its aquatic foundations.

One day, while Ezekiel lay in a fitful pseudo-sleep, Eli snuck into his father's room and took the boots—promising himself all the while that he would return them on the day they were no longer needed. Eli then tinkered with the boots until he finally had them functional. Since then, he had used them to play his shadowy trade.

Eli glanced up at the window, sizing up the jump one last time. Then he leaped out, soaring up through the air and across the dark chasm that yawned between him and the apartment building. His first target was a window ledge two floors below, and to the right of, his intended destination. The youth landed on the ledge outside of the window, his feet on either side of a flower pot that resided there. Then he turned his head to locate his intended window. Catching sight of it, he made another astounding leap and landed softly upon its ledge. Carefully, he opened the window more fully, and slipped inside.

He found himself in a small dining room, lined in a dark, richly colored wood, which gave the room a warm cozy kind of feel. There was a table directly in front of him, over which was a small decorative chandelier, and around the room were a few paintings of beautiful landscapes. Eli took this in at a glance, then moved towards a room that more readily held his attention —the kitchen. Stepping into the room he saw a wall lined with many small cabinets, beneath them was a counter top that coiled around the room, its surface occasionally interrupted by the presence of some appliance. Eli carefully, opened a few drawers and cabinets, to take stock of the abundance or scarcity within them. It was a practice Eli was firm about: before he would commit to taking from the cabinets of a house he would look through them and assess whether the family would be jeopardized by his thievery; he refused to sentence another family to starvation. These looked to be stocked quite sufficiently, and he would only be taking enough to feed him and his father for a few days. He slid a black backpack off his shoulders and began quietly filling it with supplies.

That finished, he turned to leave, but stopped as something caught his eye: a sleek refrigerator that stood resolutely in one corner. Eli hadn't paid it much mind before, because he typically didn't bother with items that needed to be kept cool, however, as he looked at it he noticed that its cold face was decorated with photos. The photos were of smiling children, laughing and playing on a sunny afternoon, and between the photos were small, colorful drawings. Eli quickly ripped his gaze away from these painful images and hurried out of the kitchen and back through the small dining room, now seemingly filled with the ghostly presence of a family, laughing and sharing a meal.

"No!" thought Eli. "Don't think about it!"

Swiftly, he walked across the room—fighting the urge to run—and slipped out the window, shutting it completely as he left.

***

Eli's heart was heavy as he began his journey home. This wasn't the first time, though. It was easy to tell yourself that the stealing was necessary, and almost even feel convinced that it was justified in this situation, but, whenever there suddenly was a face behind it—there were no words that could consolidate that. Eli Era was painfully aware that he was not the only one in this city that was hurting, and it tore him apart to think that he might spread that hurt, like some retched disease.

It was with these types of tumultuous thoughts that Eli grappled. Their weight was so great that they demanded his entire focus. Thus, he was caught by surprise when, in mid-jump, a blinding light suddenly erupted on his left. Out of reflex, he naturally turned his head in the direction of the light, and found himself blinded by it, so that, when he landed on the next roof, he missed his footing and landed hard upon his side.

"Attention: this is the police!" called a voice over a loudspeaker. "We have a warrant for your arrest. Do not resist or we will have to resort to force!"

"I've been wondering about that." thought Eli.

He knew when he started all of this that it would only be a matter of time before the law enforcement would be after him. Unfortunately, Eli had never really thought about what he would do when that time came. For a moment, Eli saw those pictures again within his mind and wondered whether it would really just be better if he simply turned himself in, but then he thought of his father, and knew that he had to get back to him.

"We're coming up!" warned the loudspeaker.

Eli, still lying on the roof, crawled over to the far edge, and took a breath before pushing himself quickly to his feet and pitching himself off the roof.

"HALT!" demanded the loudspeaker.

"Afraid not." thought Eli, as he hit the next roof and jumped for another.

Suddenly, the night skyline of Havenport was alive with action. A squadron of officers, equipped with heavy-duty grappling guns, landed upon the roof that Eli had started from and quickly pursued their intended prisoner. Their guns were designed with a strong retractable cord, made from a surprisingly light material, and on the end of this line was a powerful electro-magnet that anchored to a surface and propelled the user to it. On the ground, sirens could be heard wailing into life, as the ground units began to follow from below. From behind him, Eli thought he could hear the leader of the Grapple-gun squad make a call for air support.

Eli tried to shake them off, making some risky leaps and even briefly ducking down into the shadowy alleys on the ground below, but nothing could throw the squadron off. Eli knew that he would have to think of something; soon they would reach the Northeast corner of the city and he would be trapped in a corner. He was debating what his next move should be, when suddenly, as he landed on the next roof, his feet shot out from under him and the whole roof seemed to explode into motion as officers poured out of their hiding places. Sprawled out on his back, Eli took in the whole situation in an instant: the officers had laid a dark tarp of some kind on the roof and yanked it out from under him when he'd landed on it, and now they were rushing forward to subdue him. As the first officer came up to him, Eli had an idea. With both feet, Eli kicked at the man as hard as he could, which, with his gravitational-boots, resulted in the officer being thrown back onto his companions while Eli was propelled across the surface of the roof, away from their numbers. As he came to a stop, Eli rolled to his feet and turned to jump to the safety of the next roof, but checked himself when he noticed that the roof was held by the Grapple-gun squad, who had circled around so as to trap him. Eli sought for an escape, but behind him the city ended abruptly, leaving only a steep descent into the ocean. Eli was cornered.

"It's over, lad!" called an officer, whose ornate badge denoted him as a man of rank. "You'd best give it up here; just take that mask off."

"I'm afraid not, officer." said Eli.

"Well, what do you think you're gonna do?" asked the officer.

Eli didn't reply but, instead, turned and threw himself from the roof in the direction of the sea. The air shrieked past Eli as he fell toward the water, which seemed like an immense gray wall, on which he would be dashed to pieces. He readjusted himself so that he would land in the water feet first, in the hopes of reducing the surface impact. As the water drew near, Eli took in a deep breath and closed his eyes, waiting for the dark waters to engulf him. However, it never came.

Curious, Eli opened his eyes and, to his amazement, found that he was standing on what appeared to be a vast plain of gray that gently rose and fell—the ocean. For a moment Eli was confused, but the answer became clear when he glanced down at his feet.

"The boots!" thought Eli, as he laughed aloud, "Their properties must keep me from breaking the surface tension of the water, just as the same technology does for the city!"

Unfortunately, Eli did not have long to dwell on this fascinating discovery, because at that time he was distracted by a low-humming that filled the air. Eli looked up and saw a large helicopter descending towards him from the city—air support had arrived. Eli looked about, wondering where he could run to. He decided to seek shelter under the city, reasoning that though the gravitational technology held the city high enough for him to easily maneuver under, it would be risky to fly the larger air unit down there. Eli set out with caution, grimacing at the thought of what should happen if he tripped. The first steps were awkward and shaky, almost resulting in a catastrophic capsizing. The surface of the water was unlike anything Eli had ever tried to walk on: for the most part it was slick, like ice, but it rolled and dipped as waves came by. Eli quickly decided that the best method was to either skip along the surface, or treat it like ice-skating (he was not sure how he would stop quickly). As he got under the shelter of the city, Eli ventured a glance back at the air unit, and saw that he was correct: it seemed reluctant to follow him under the city. However, Eli also saw that it wasn't going to simply give-up there. The air unit was dispatching its drones.

There were five of them, all equipped with a large claw, used as a full-body handcuff on the intended target.

Eli skipped across the water as fast as he could, all the while searching the machinery above him until his gaze landed on what he had been seeking: a small suspended bridge, used by the maintenance crews that tended to this complex technology. Eli gathered himself and put all his strength into the jump, but the bridge was still out of his reach. For a moment, panic seized him as he wondered how he would escape, but then he had an idea.

Eli turned to face the oncoming drones and took a breath to steady himself; this was going to take skill. The drones swarmed towards him, closing the distance between them with a terrifying speed. Eli forced himself to wait; he stood upon the water and faced the swarm. Then, just before they reached him, he leaped forward, propelling himself into the swarm of low-humming drones. His eyes were locked on one specific drone: the one that was coming directly at him. Right before they collided, Eli raised his feet and kicked off from the drone. The drone was sent spiraling through the air, crashing into one of its compatriots and taking both down into the darkness of the ocean. Eli flew through the air, landing lightly upon the maintenance bridge. He made a mental note that that was likely the coolest thing he would ever do in his life, then he turned to flee, as the remaining three drones would soon be upon him. Eli crossed the bridge and found a door leading back toward the surface; he ducked into it, leaving the angry buzz of the drones behind him.

***

Quietly, Eli slipped into the apartment. By this time his father was likely asleep. He stored the food in the kitchen and started toward his room, thinking eagerly of a good night's rest. He got to the end of the hallway and was frozen to the spot as he came face to face with his father.

Ezekiel Era was a powerfully built man, though his degenerative disease had taken a toll upon him, now sentencing him to dependence on a wheelchair. However, strength comes in many forms, and, for now, this disease did not affect all of them. Ezekiel was still undeniably keen in mind, and in his eyes one could still recognize his strength of character; prepared to help others find the way, despite whatever disaster life may bring. It was these eyes that now looked upon Eli, and Eli couldn't help but think they seemed even now to be sizing up life's latest disaster.

Silence hung in the air. Finally, Ezekiel reached over to the broadcasting stand and pressed a button, causing the hologram display to come to life. It was a news feed, displaying the latest footage of the current top story. Eli grimaced at the images it presented. First there was a shot of a dark-clad figure hopping across the rooftops with a squadron of officers following behind, then there was a shot of the figure skating across the water, and there was also some drone footage of the figure leaping off the water and kicking off from another drone, but the worst one was a short clip of an officer being taken up in an emergency air unit, while another officer, wearing an ornate badge, talked to the camera.

"—we won't rest until this terror is stopped," he was saying.

This was more than Eli's troubled heart could take. His hand lashed out and hit a button on the broadcasting stand, shutting off the awful images.

"Why?" asked Ezekiel, in a low deliberate tone.

"Because I had to." replied Eli weakly.

"And so you stole my prototype and used it to rob others of their hard-earned bread." continued Ezekiel. "Aren't there enough sorrows in Havenport without that?"

Eli took a shaky breath, thinking of the pictures on that refrigerator. "Then what would you have me do?" he asked, miserably.

Ezekiel was silent for a moment before answering. "I would have you give to these people, instead of take from them." he stated.

"DO YOU THINK I LIKE THIS?!" cried Eli. "I want to stop this whole miserable business!"

"Then join with me, and we can end it together." said Ezekiel.

Eli studied his father with some skepticism. "What do you mean?" he asked.

"I mean, we are going to fix this. And we're only going to do that by getting to the root of the whole wretched problem." stated Ezekiel.

"How do you intend for us to do that? The whole city tried to do that during The Stagnation." questioned Eli, though he couldn't help but be interested.

"That's just it," said Ezekiel, "they all tried to keep that same department on its feet. But that's not what we're doing; we are going to start something new." Ezekiel let those words hang in the air before continuing, "I think I'm on the trail of a final cure for my sickness. If I can perfect it, then we'll be ready to make our first move."

Eli sat down in a chair across from his father, trying to process this feeling he had that they were on the cusp of something monumental. He shook his head and grinned at his father.

"Alright," he said, with a laugh, "I'm in. All this," he gestured at his backpack, holding the boots and dark clothes, "is over; I'm done with it."

Ezekiel leaned forward. "Eli... son," he said, choosing his words carefully, "we're going to help this whole city. But to do that I need to finish this antidote, which requires just a little more time. We have to get by till then..."

"But, I thought you disapproved?" Eli said incredulously.

"I do," replied his father. "Unfortunately, necessity drives us to it: I need you to play the thief for just a while longer."

A heavy silence fell upon the room, as Eli wrestled with the turmoil of images within his mind: the smiling children, the officer being taken in the emergency air unit, and the officer with the ornate badge. A terror, that's what he was.

"How could I justify continuing that?!" he thought.

Ezekiel leaned forward; concerned by the effect this news seemed to be having on his son. "This city needs us." said Ezekiel.

Fortune's Veil

By: J. Riley Peak

FORTUNE'S VEIL

With a grunt, the young man stood to his feet and stretched, observing his surroundings as his did so. He was standing on the shale-strewn banks of a river in the bottom of a low valley. The land looked ravaged by war, upturned and riddled with many holes all along the valley. The young man gazed up and down the valley, assessing the abundance of this destruction.

“Quite a bit for one day," he thought.

Of course, he had to concede that he hadn’t done it all on his own. There were many others digging in this valley, the dull reverberating tempo of their tools echoed throughout the hills, bearing witness to their presence just around the bend. It was the later part of the day here along the American river and the golden California sun was beating down mercilessly upon the land and all its unfortunate laborers. It was another drought season.

“Better get back at it,” he said, scooping up his pickaxe and shovel.

He proceeded down the bank a ways till he came to what he gauged to be a good spot, and, more importantly, one that would be shaded sooner by the tree line on the valley rim. It was another hot day out here in Fortune’s Vale. The young man took note of that as he wiped the sweat from his brow and tossed his shovel to one side.

"Just one more hole, then we'll call it a day," he thought.

He squared up, hoisted his pickaxe back, and brought it forth in a mighty stroke, plunging it deep into the soil. The action, reminded him of chopping wood. However, he felt that the uses of the pickaxe reminded him more of a hoe. As he continued to break up the ground with it, he found his mind drifting back to the home he had left behind, and the events of that last day he had made use of gardening tools.

***

It was in the summer of 1851. He, Hoyt Caldale, had been hoeing out the weeds in the garden and had just started into the corn.

The scene was beautiful. The sun shined across the tops of the willowy stalks, and the sky was a deep blue. Hoyt was working with his two younger brothers, Thomas and Buck. Hoyt's younger sister, Jenny, was outside as well. Normally, the boys' sister would be inside helping their mother with chores there but Jenny had been complaining about feeling rather ill that morning so their mother had recommended that she go out and get some fresh air while her brothers were tending to the garden. As the siblings had set out, their mother had pulled Hoyt aside and whispered additional instructions to him, telling him to keep an eye on his sister.

Now, as Hoyt and his two younger brothers were nearing the end of their task, Hoyt cast his gaze around for his sister. He turned and, looking past his brothers, saw her, lingering on the other side of the field, in the shade of a few oaks.

“Do you think she’s alright?” asked Thomas, turning to follow Hoyt’s gaze.

“I don’t really know,” answered Hoyt. “I fear she’s coming down with something.”

“Yeah, that’s for sure,” said Buck, the youngest of the family. “Think it’s the stomach bug that Howard’s sister had last week?”

“I don’t see how it could be, Buck,” answered Thomas. “Jenny ain’t been anywhere near Howard’s sister.”

The two younger brothers, now completely distracted from the hoeing, continued to debate what the illness could be. Hoyt, turned to scold them back to work, but his words caught in his mouth as, looking past his brothers, he was just in time to see Jenny collapse to the soft, green grass. The brothers had rushed to their sister, and Hoyt had carried her to the house while the younger two swiftly ran for the doctor. The boys had returned with Doctor Crowner just as Hoyt finished explaining to his mother what had happened. While the doctor and Mrs. Caldale tended to Jenny, the boys had waited outside, waiting distractedly for any news. Then Mrs. Caldale had come out on the porch and asked Hoyt to come inside with her and the doctor. Hoyt obeyed and was soon sitting in the living room with his mother and Doctor Crowner.

“Doctor Crowner says it doesn’t look good,” began Mrs. Caldale, taking a shaky breath. “He says it’s not just some kind of bug; it’s a long-term illness, and a serious one. He said that, without treatment, Jenny could--” she broke off, her voice choking.

“Hoyt,” said Doctor Crowner, taking up for Mrs. Caldale, “your sister is in danger.”

“Isn’t there something we can do?” asked Hoyt.

“There is,” said the doctor. “However, it’s expensive. I’ve been talking it over with your mother, and here’s the dilemma: you can cover the first dose of this treatment, but, when the second one is needed, you won’t be able to afford it—”

“So you’ll let her die because we can’t pay you?” interjected Hoyt, a cold spark in his eyes.

“It’s not that, Hoyt,” the doctor said gently, “the problem is that I can’t afford the medicine without that pay; you know my family doesn’t have much either.” The doctor waited till Hoyt backed down before beginning again. “As I was saying, I and Mrs. Caldale have been discussing the issue, and we think we’ve found a solution. However, Hoyt, since your father has passed away, leaving you as the man of the household, I’m afraid the brunt of this task will fall on you.”

“Name it,” said the young man, a determined air settling about his features.

“Very well,” said the doctor, nodding his approval. “You’re to go to California. They say men have already dug fortunes out of that land—and their still finding more. That would be just the thing we need.”

“But how could that work?” asked Hoyt.

“Well, the vaccine I will give your sister will not require a second dose for another year,” said Doctor Crowner. “Meaning you have that long to strike gold and bring it home.” The doctor allowed that to sink in before beginning again. “Now, there are several ways to get to California, but only one will meet our schedule: you are to sail down through the Caribbean and crossing the jungles of Panama, then sail on to California—arriving there in one month, if all goes smoothly.”

“And how am I to pay for that?” asked Hoyt.

The doctor smiled. “I have a fellow of who owes me for a past favor, and he just so happens to own a ship. I believe he could arrange for you to work your way over.”

And so, one week later, Hoyt and Doctor Crowner stood upon the quays around the moored vessel, Providence. As Hoyt prepared to board, the doctor grabbed his shoulder and pressed something into his hand. Hoyt was shocked to find it was a wad of cash.

“I thought you said you and your family were in it rather tight?” Hoyt said with skepticism.

“I did. And we are,” stated the doctor. “That,” he said, pointing at Hoyt’s hand, “is from the whole town. I didn’t tell your mother that you will have to pay when you change ships after crossing Panama. That cash is for securing that voyage—and perhaps enough to barter your way onto a ship quickly—guard it with your life.”

***

Night was coming upon Fortune’s Vale, and Hoyt figured it was time to head back to camp. He gathered up his tools and began the long weary hike. Upon entering the camp, Hoyt was greeted by the usual scene: men talking loudly of their homeland; others, who had been at strong drink, were talking loudly of nothing at all; and another group used their weathered instruments to strike up a bouncy tune, to which, several men danced around. It seemed a scene of merriment, and matched the glamorized images that many young men came over here bearing in mind about the prospector’s life, but Hoyt had been here long enough to see right through the surface of this façade. These men engaged in this all-in sort of gaiety simply to hide from the emotion they really felt—bitter loneliness.

This pseudo-joy, however, wasn't the only emotion running high at that time; from the other side of the camp, an angry voice could be heard. Hoyt looked through the crowd and saw the source of this discontent: a pair of men. One of the fellows seemed to believe that the other had stolen from his tent and was very vociferous about his dislike of this. The other seemed to be replying with equally voluble phrases, until the first fellow decided it prompt to oblige his acquaintance to be silent, which he did with a smart punch to the nose.

Hoyt grimaced at the blow, his hand drifting involuntarily to his own nose, as the scene brought to his mind another memory of the past.

***

The work upon the Providence had not been hard. Hoyt primarily worked around the dining room of the ship, cleaning tables and washing dishes. He had been doing this for several days with no trouble, but then, one evening, as he was leaving the kitchens, Hoyt walked out of the kitchens and bumped straight into a solid wall (which, upon closer inspection, he realized was a man).

"Thought you could get away with it, eh?" growled the man, his accent denoting him as a man from the north.

"With what?" asked Hoyt, fully aware that he was looking up at the man.

The man didn't even seem to register the question, instead he continued his steady growl.

"One moment, my pocket watch is on the table, then you come by to clean a table and the watch disappears."

A crowd of interested bystanders was now gathering.

"What are you trying to say, sir?" asked Hoyt.

"THIEVERY AIN'T TAKEN LIGHTLY!" roared the man.

Hoyt saw, but was not swift enough to dodge, the sledgehammer-fist aimed straight at his face. It lifted him off his feet and threw him to the floor in a crumpled heap.

"Check him," the man grunted to a few fellows standing around. "He should have my watch in his pockets."

Hoyt, in his dazed state, was only dimly aware of the men checking his pockets.

"No watch. But he does have this," he heard one of the men saying.

"Hmm, must have hid it in the kitchens," said the hulking individual. "However, I'll consider that as repayment for his crimes. Hand it over."

Hoyt was wondering what the man could have found in his pockets, then felt his heart jump into his throat, as he realized what it was. Opening his eyes, he found he was correct —the man had the roll of cash that Doctor Crowner had given him.

"Give that back," groaned Hoyt, getting shakily to his feet.

The man cast a disdainful eye at Hoyt. "I'm sure you could get enough from selling my pocket watch," he said.

"Give it back," Hoyt repeated, trying hard to get some steel in his voice.

"Oh-ho! Lookout, Victor, I think the lad's gonna come after you," said someone in the crowd.

"Yeah, best guard your pockets; he might take something else!" called another.

The colossal northerner put the wad of cash into his pocket, and smiled at Hoyt, though, Hoyt noted, it wasn't a kind sort of smile.

"Come on, lad. I'll break every bone in that thievin' hand of yours."

Hoyt, swallowed dryly, as he stood before the towering figure of Victor. By this point, he had decided that the man must be a lumberjack, whose job was either to simply push trees over with his hulking frame or to clear the logged land by pushing the stumps into the ground with his little finger. Hoyt was scared, and still dizzy from the last blow he had taken. However, Hoyt was also headstrong, twenty-year-old farm boy, who never really thought such things all the way through. Thus, the first fist was thrown without a second thought.

Victor easily dodged the punch, stepping back out of the way. Then, the logger stepped in to throw a punch of his own: a massive, freight-train-right-hook. This time, Hoyt was ready. He ducked, allowing the fist to sail by overhead, then he awkwardly threw himself back, as Victor immediately followed his right hook with a left-handed uppercut. A few enthusiasts, who had joined the crowd around the fighters, caught Hoyt and threw him back onto his feet in the improvised ring that had formed. Victor met Hoyt with another fist, which Hoyt dodged by a desperate dive to the floor. A few fellows on the edges prompted Hoyt back to his feet with a few swift kicks. Once he was back upright, Hoyt tried to go back on the offensive, but Victor slapped his fist dismissively out of the air, and sent Hoyt back to the floor with one solid blow to the head. Hoyt was out cold.

When he came back to, Hoyt found himself bandaged and lying on a bed. He tried to sit up, but quickly decided that it wouldn't be a good investment.

"Well, you're brave; I'll grant you that," said a voice.

Hoyt turned and saw a man sitting in a chair by the window on the other side of the small room. He looked to be only a little older than Hoyt.

"However," he continued, "I do believe you bit off more than you could chew."

"I suppose you could say that," said Hoyt through a cracked smile, his voice thick. "But, it doesn't matter," he sighed, "I lost more than just a fight there."

"I noticed that," said the young man, getting up and crossing over to the bed, "and that's why I stepped in. Here, I believe this is yours."

And, to Hoyt's amazement, the man handed him the money that had come from Doctor Crowner.

"My name's Daniel."

***

Hoyt shrugged off the thoughts as he sat down to his meager supper on the edge of the camp. It was his habit to sit out here, using the gorgeous scenery in an attempt to pay as little attention to the vile gruel he was consuming.

It was a beautiful landscape. The camp was on the south rim of the valley, and this perch allowed a clear view down the length of the American river. Under the night sky, the river seemed like a strip of liquid silver, flowing off toward some crystal sea. The dark face of the sky was freckled with many brilliant stars, causing it to blush a clear white light. Hoyt took a deep breath of the clean night air and wondered if these were the same stars he had watched from his home. It was comforting to think that perhaps here was one thing that tied him back to the place he had left.

Finishing his meal, Hoyt decided it was time to seek out a few hours of sleep. He rose from his position and, casting one last look over the luminous valley and the star-speckled sky, made his way back into the camp.

Hoyt's tent, like the majority of all the others in the camp, was a simple one man structure, made from a pine branch frame, a few homemade stakes, and a tattered sheet. He crawled into the structure and threw his boots over to one side, with his other meager possessions. Hoyt pulled out a grubby piece of paper and a small stub of pencil. The paper had a long list of small boxes, each with a blank line beside it. Several boxes were already marked, most with an 'X', but a few had check marks within them. Looking over the list, Hoyt sighed and scrawled an 'X' in the next box on the list, scribbling a zero in the blank beside the box.

"Another empty day," he thought bitterly.

He'd been here over a month and had relatively little to show for it.

"I don't even have enough to pay my way back home yet," he thought, checking the figures on the list in exasperation.

With a sigh, he returned the paper and pencil to their place and stretched himself out on the floor. Despite his troubled mind, Hoyt soon was drifting off to sleep, his subconscious filling with scenes of the past.

***

"Hoyt, come check this out!"

It was Daniel, calling from the rails of the ship. Over the last two days of the voyage, Daniel and Hoyt had spent the majority of their time (when Hoyt wasn't working) together, quickly forming a friendship between the two.

Hoyt, who had been mopping the deck, put down his bucket and, mop still in hand, came to see what had excited his friend. As he reached the rail, he saw a green mass rising over the far horizon.

"The jungles of Panama," stated Daniel.

Suddenly, the scene seemed to shift. Now, Hoyt was on the coast following the crowd as they entered the jungle.

"Stay in close, lads," called the guide from his position in the front. "There's danger of all sorts within these here jungles: animals, Spanish raiders, and..." he didn't say what the last group was, but instead turned and looked back at the group, saying, "we'll just hope we don't meet them."

The group marched into the shadows cast by the dense jungle canopy. Hoyt cast his wary eye all around at this alien world full of mysterious dangers. It seemed terrifying, the very plants around him appeared to be closing in, and the air was systematically split by the shrieks of strange creatures—causing Hoyt to leap in fright.

They trekked on and on, for what seemed like an eternity. Hoyt felt as though his legs were about to give out, but the guide was still moving along at a brisk pace. If Hoyt stopped, he knew he would quickly be left behind.

Thus, Hoyt continued to stumble on. But, despite his efforts, he seemed to be growing slower and slower; finding it harder to stay with the group. It was like he had something weighing him down, but he didn't know what. It was then that Hoyt became aware of a hand upon his shoulder and realized that he was indeed bearing an extra weight; someone was pulling him back. Afraid, he pushed the hand away, and heard a low, troubled moan come from behind him. Turning around, Hoyt felt a coat of ice line his stomach as he saw Daniel, his friend, lying balled up on the ground, unable to move. Hoyt dropped to the ground, calling for help from the front as he did so.

The guide was soon there and, with a worried look on his face, gave Daniel a quick examination. After a moment, he uttered a quiet curse and stood to his feet.

"It's the Yellow Jack, lad; you won't be savin' him," he said, grabbing Hoyt and attempting to drag him back to the group. "We'd best be moving on."

"No, that's my friend; you don't understand," cried Hoyt. "YOU CAN'T LEAVE HIM!"

But, the guide and the rest of the group seemed to have every intention of doing just that. They continued to drag Hoyt away from his friend. Hoyt resisted, his gaze locked on the writhing figure of Daniel. The forest now seemed to echo with Daniels low, continuous moan.

"It's them!" squawked the guide. "It's the Stranded! RUN!"

Hoyt watched in horror as shaky forms stumbled out of the jungle, all pinched and sickly; pleading for help and rescue. They, like Daniel had fallen sick, and were abandoned in this jungle. Now they sought to latch themselves to any passerby, in the hopes of being brought out from their wanderings.

Quaking in distilled terror, Hoyt tore out off the grip of his companions, who had been dragging him, and started to join their flight. However, Hoyt found that his friends had not been dragging him; instead he saw five pale-faced, moaning Stranded, who had been in the process of dragging him into the jungle. With a cry, Hoyt fled from his would-be captors. As he ran down the trail, hands stretched out on all sides to catch him, but he struggled through them. Hoyt thought he screamed the whole way, but the incessant moaning drowned out all noise; it rang in his ears and pressed him to run faster. Then, Hoyt saw the end; it was gilded in wondrous sunlight. As he reached it, he ventured one last look back, and stopped. All was still. The Stranded had disappeared, and in their place was one small figure, unimaginably small against the oppressive backdrop of the jungle. Hoyt's heart seemed to die as he recognized the figure. Jenny.

***

Hoyt awoke with a hoarse cry. He was bathed in a cold sweat, his heart racing. The fabric of his tent glowed with a pale light, telling him that it was dawn. Still trembling, Hoyt sat up and put on his boots. Then he threw open the tent and stepped out into the dawn. Walking over to the edge of camp, Hoyt surveyed the American river valley. There was a cold mist slithering along the valley.

Hoyt stood there shivering, but was uncertain whether he was doing so because of the cool wind that was blowing or the image of that small figure in the jungle which was still so clear in his mind.

Time for another day.

The Economic Endeavors of Orval and Rufus

By: J. Riley Peak

THE ECONOMIC ENDEAVORS OF ORVAL AND RUFUS

ACT 1
SCENE 1

Setting: *A street in front of a factory in London in the year 1827.*

[Scuffling heard from within factory. Doors burst open as Orval and Rufus are tossed headlong out of the factory by Boss, who looks very angry.]

Boss:
Fired! Both of you! And don't even think about stepping one foot back in here, or you'll be thrown from the second story instead of the first!

[slams door shut.]

Orval:

[Getting to his feet.]

Why, the nerve of that man! Anyone with a brain could have seen that our methods would have improved the factories speed to its utmost capacity; we simply needed a few more trousers.

Rufus:

[Still lying on the ground, moaning.]

Oh, but Orval, now we're fired! We have to start all over and find new jobs!

Orval:

Find new jobs?!

[Dropping down on his hands and knees beside Rufus.]

Rufus, we have been wronged by the system! Are we simply puppets within its clutches, so that we merely follow its every bidding? No!

[jumps back to feet. Working himself up.]

I'll say it again: we have been wronged by the system! And, in our case, the only right for us is to wrong them with an equally wrong sort of wrong.

Rufus:

[Stands up. Unable to keep up with Orval's ravings.]

What do you mean, Orval?

Orval:

We are turning to a life of crime!

Rufus:

[Expression never changes.]

But Orval, there're such nice people around here.

Orval:

Don't think on it Rufus! You'll lose your nerve if you start thinking like that. Our objective is to remain equally cold and ruthless towards all, disregarding their amount of connection with our plight.

Rufus:

[Nodding his understanding.]

Alright, Orval.

[pause.]

So, where do we start?

Orval:

[Cringing at what he sees as such a rhetorical question.]

Why, where there's people, of course! Really Rufus, you should think before you speak.

[Stopping Rufus before he can open his mouth to ask another question.]

No more! Follow me, and you will understand.

[Orval exits.]

Rufus:

[shrugging his shoulders.]

I'll follow, but I'm not sure I'll ever understand.

[Rufus exits.]

ACT 1
SCENE 2

Setting: *A park, midday. People are strolling around.*

[Orval and Rufus enter.]

Orval:

[Spreading his arms wide.]

Ah, here we are: the perfect location for our sort. We should find our work quite simple in this sort of crowd.

Rufus:

Orval, what exactly are we doing?

Orval:

[Cringes. Starts to rebuke Rufus for foolish questions then decides to spare Rufus this time.]

We are engaging in the common income of every criminal in this town: pickpocketing.

Rufus:

How do we do that, Orval? Shouldn't we practice first?

Orval:

Rufus! This is the commonest sort of thing in the business! If we can't pull this off, we might as well throw in our glittering careers. Honestly, how hard could it be? Rather like picking cabbage, I suppose.

[Points at Sgt. Wilbur, who is strolling by.]

And there's our first subject—ripe for the picking, judging by his apparel.

[Leans over and whispers to Rufus.]

Here's the plan: I'll take the front and distract the chap; you come from behind and harvest his pockets.

Rufus:

[Weakly.]

Orval, I don't know if I can do this...

Orval:

No time for such pessimism, Rufus. It's time to start our new business venture!

[runs to catch up with Sgt. Wilbur, then falls into a "casual" pace beside him. Orval looks over and acts as though he has just noticed Sgt. Wilbur.]

Oh, good day, sir! And how is your day in this fine establishment treating you today?

[Casts a large wink back at Rufus]

Sgt. Wilbur:

[Noticing Orval.]

What's that? Oh, quite delightful, I should say. Yes, rather splendid, in fact.

Orval:

How nice.

[Blatantly stepping in front of Sgt. Wilbur, placing the man between Orval and Rufus and forcing him to stop his walking.]

And what brings you here today?

Sgt. Wilbur:

Why, it's my particular custom; I always come to this park at precisely 1:47pm every day.

Orval:

[making "subtle" gesture for Rufus to move in. Rufus shakes his head and shifts his feet.]

Is that so?

[Orval continues to make increasingly less "subtle" gestures at Rufus, with Rufus persisting in his nervous refusal to act, as Sgt. Wilbur says next line.]

Sgt. Wilbur:

Certainly! It's quite irregular if I don't.

[pulls out a schedule from his pocket.]

You see I keep a very tight schedule; if I were to stray in the slightest detail, why, I should say I would be behind for the rest of the week!

Orval:

[snapping back to attention.]

Oh yes, that would be a bother.

Sgt. Wilbur:

[Returning the schedule to his pocket.]

Most assuredly. It's a bothersome load at times, but I find that maintaining a tight operation is the only way to get things done.

Orval:

Right you are, my dear fellow!

[Orval casts a venomous look over Sgt. Wilbur, at Rufus, as he says the next line.]

There's a lot to be learned in that type of doctrine: getting things done!

[Emphasis on the words "getting things done".]

Sgt. Wilbur:

Quite right!

[Reminiscing.]

Why, back in the army, that was always the first thing I put into those lads: how to accomplish something with those hands of theirs!

Orval:

Certainly! They all needed to know how to

[looks up at Rufus.]

SCOOP UP THEIR LILY-LACED HEARTS, AND DO SOMETHING WITH THEIR HANDS!

Sgt. Wilbur:

[Oblivious. Nodding his head at memories.]

Quite right.

Orval:

[Begins to walk away. Speaks to Sgt. Wilbur, but his disgusted gaze is set on Rufus.]

Pardon me, but I'm sure you're running late for something or another.

Sgt. Wilbur:

[Stirring from his memories.]

Eh, what? Oh!

[Pulls schedule from pocket.]

Great Scott! I'm nearly behind schedule!

[Runs through the park, knocking people aside.]

Make way! I'm late! CHARGE!!!

[Sgt. Wilbur exits.]

Orval:

[Walks over to Rufus. Sums up his disgust.]

Rufus, you ninny.

ACT 2
SCENE 1

Setting: *In Rufus' house. The room is simple, with a sofa against the right side of the back wall; beside it is a small table. Thrown across the floor is a large, decidedly ugly, carpet. On the left side of the back wall is a door.*

[Rufus enters, walking through the room when a swift, sharp, knock is heard upon the door.]

Rufus:

[Moves towards the door.]

Coming!

[Opens door. Orval enters through it.]

Orval:

Top of the morning, Rufus!

Rufus:

Hello, Orval. Would you like some—

Orval:

[Motions for Rufus to hold his small talk.]

Hush, we have more important things to tend to. I spent half the night pondering my intellect upon our precise predicament, and I have found a solution to our economic deficiencies that even a spineless individual like you should be able to contribute in.

Rufus:

[Embarrassed at the mention of his failure of the previous day.]

What's that, Orval?

Orval:

Street-side performance!

[Stated triumphantly.]

Rufus:

Orval, I don't know if we should—

Orval:

[Cutting him off.]

Rufus, this is not the place for more of your pessimism. I have done my research on this topic, and feel that we shall excel at it. Now, follow me.

[Opens door.]

Rufus:

To where, Orval?

Orval:

[Taken aback by such a foolish question.]

Why, Rufus, we cannot be street-side performers without a proper street-side. Come along now!

[Orval and Rufus exit through the door.]

ACT 2
SCENE 2

Setting: *A busy Street in London. People move about, tending to their daily tasks. A shopkeeper is perched precariously atop a lightly framed ladder, attempting to hang up a bulky sign for his shop. Further down, a man sits with his back against the buildings, playing a twangy sounding instrument. A man strolls around the street with a wheelbarrow of produce, seeking to sell his wares.*

[Orval and Rufus enter.]

Orval:
I would think that this should do just fine; we'll set up shop here, Rufus.

Rufus:
[looking around the street.]
Orval, precisely how does this work?

Orval:
[Excited.]
It's quite fascinating: we simply engage in some elaborate spectacle, and people give us money!
[Shakes head.]
It's absolutely extraordinary what people will do these days.

Rufus:
[Still nervous.]
Could we get into trouble?

Orval:

[Waving his hand dismissively.]

Pish posh! I've been observing this phenomenon all morning! I went out at the break of dawn, so as to establish myself in full camouflage before the arrival of the skilled artisans of this trade. When they began their work, I observed the customs involved in this kind of labor. I should have within my intellect all the knowledge required for our success.

[They move to the side of the street.]

Rufus:

[Slightly reassured.]

Alright. Well, what do we do first?

Orval:

First, we set up shop.

[Reaches into coat and withdraws a small wooden box, which he places upon the ground between them.]

Right.

[Straightening back up.]

Now we perform.

Rufus:

[Nodding his head.]

And what're we going to do, Orval?

Orval:

[Looks up at Rufus, with an expression of blank thought, then smiles.]

That, dear fellow, is where you come in.

Rufus:

[Frightened.]

Me?! But how should I know what to perform? I'm no actor!

Orval:

[Quick to reassure him.]

And that's why you will succeed. You're looking at this the wrong way, Rufus.

[Sweeps arm in the direction of the people going down the street.]

These people don't want an act, they want true talent! They want to see how you exploit the raw resources and potential which you have within yourself. They want the show; they want to be your first fans.

Rufus:

[Eyes bulging.]

Really?

[Orval nods.]

Wow.

Orval:

So then, what do you say?

Rufus:

[Straightening up. Speaks with a new confidence.]

Just follow my lead.

Orval:

[Caught off-guard by the sudden change in his friend.]

There's a good lad.

[Rufus takes a deep breath, then bounces and stomps out a beats. He then gestures to Orval, who mirrors his companions display, and passes it back to Rufus upon completion. Rufus continues the phenomenon, making it more elaborate, then passes it back. The two of them pass it back and forth for a time, then launch into it together. The man down the street with the instrument notices the dancing and strikes up a tempo to match their dance, and leads the dancers to increase the speed. The people in the street walk by without the slightest interest.]

Rufus:

[Still dancing. Nodding his head toward the people on the street.]

They don't seem to be interested!

Orval:

[Still dancing.]

Then we shall employ the tactics of the trade—taking the show to them! Follow me!

[Orval and Rufus begin to dance their way out into the street, but, as they proceed, Orval bumps into the ladder of the precariously perched shopkeeper, causing the shopkeeper to fall off the ladder and straight into the wheelbarrow of the produce salesman.]

Orval:

[Grabbing Rufus, who is still dancing.]

Spot on performance, my friend. However, I now feel that a vanishing act is in order!

[Orval and Rufus run off stage.]

ACT 2
SCENE 3

Setting: *Quays of London. Barrels and various cargos sit around.*
[Orval and Rufus enter, panting.]

Orval:
Well, that could have turned ugly.

Rufus:
Oh, but Orval, we still didn't make anything!

Orval:
Rufus, you really should do something about that pessimism of yours, it's quite exasperating!
[Conceding.]
However, you've assessed the issue rather precisely—we are still very firmly in a hole.

Rufus:
What should we do next, Orval?

Orval:
[Sighs.]
I don't know, old chap; I'm afraid I'm quite washed out at this point.
[Sits heavily upon a coil of ropes.]
Perhaps we should just throw in the towel; go back to being ill-fated puppets of the system.

Rufus:

[Sadly.]

If you say so, Orval.

Orval:

It's a sad fate, but who are we to argue? It is simply our lot in life, I suppose.

[Orval rises from his seat. He and Rufus start to leave, but the sound of a steamboat horn off stage draws Orval's attention. He stops and stares off stage at it for a moment, then runs to Rufus.]

Orval:

[Taking Rufus by the shoulder.]

Rufus, old boy, how do you feel about America?

[Rufus stares at Orval in confusion for a moment. Orval points back off stage at the steamboat. Rufus stares at it for a moment, then a smile spreads across his face as he understands.]

Rufus:

I think it sounds alright.

[Orval and Rufus run off stage in the direction of the steamboat.]

S.C. TreeHouse

www.sctreehouse.com

www.ingramcontent.com/pod-product-compliance
Lightning Source LLC
Chambersburg PA
CBHW060612310726
48982CB00003B/529

* 9 7 8 0 6 9 2 8 7 1 5 7 7 *